LOS ANGELES · NEW YORK

Written by Ella Patrick
Illustrated by PowerStation, Pilot Studio, & Leigh Zieske
Designed by Leigh Zieske



Printed in the United States of America

First Edition, July 2019

1 3 5 7 9 10 8 6 4 2

Library of Congress Control Number on file

FAC-038091-19158

ISBN 978-1-368-04341-0

Visit the official *Star Wars* website at: www.starwars.com.

Logo Applies to Text Stock Only

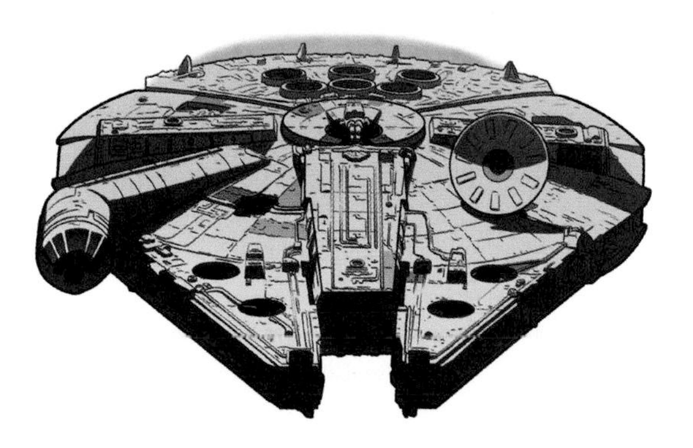

A long time ago in a galaxy far,
far away. . . .

# STAR WARS™

## THE PHANTOM MENACE

# QUI-GON JINN

Jedi Master

**Qui-Gon Jinn** is a Jedi Master. The Jedi use a mystical energy field called the Force, and laser swords called lightsabers, to protect the galaxy from harm.

# OBI-WAN KENOBI

Jedi Padawan

**Obi-Wan Kenobi** is a Jedi Padawan learner. A Padawan is a young Jedi in training.

## NUTE GUNRAY

Viceroy

**Nute Gunray** is a leader of the Trade Federation. The Trade Federation is a dangerous group that wants to control the galaxy. Nute Gunray and his droid army are keeping food and supplies from reaching a peaceful planet called Naboo—and they have captured Naboo's queen!

## DARTH SIDIOUS

Sith Lord

**Darth Sidious** is an evil Sith Lord who wants to take over the galaxy. The Sith use the dark side of the Force to hurt others. It is Darth Sidious who is giving orders to the Trade Federation officials.

Qui-Gon Jinn and Obi-Wan Kenobi try to convince the Trade Federation officials to leave Naboo alone. But Darth Sidious orders the officials to attack the Jedi with droid soldiers.

# JAR JAR BINKS

## Gungan

**Jar Jar Binks** is a friendly Gungan alien who helps Qui-Gon Jinn and Obi-Wan Kenobi hide from the Trade Federation.

# GUNGANS

## Amphibious Aliens

The **Gungans** live in the waters of Naboo. They are friendly aliens, but they do not want to fight the Trade Federation.

The Gungans give Qui-Gon Jinn and Obi-Wan Kenobi a submarine so they can secretly travel through the planet to rescue the captured queen. Obi-Wan pilots the submarine away from dangerous sea beasts!

# QUEEN AMIDALA

Queen of Naboo

**Queen Amidala** is the leader of Naboo. She wants the Trade Federation to leave her planet alone. Qui-Gon Jinn and Obi-Wan Kenobi rescue Queen Amidala from Nute Gunray and his droid army on Naboo.

# R2-D2

Astromech Droid

**R2-D2** is a clever astromech droid. R2-D2 helps Qui-Gon Jinn and Obi-Wan Kenobi rescue Queen Amidala. But their starship is damaged as they zoom away from Naboo, so the heroes must land on the remote planet Tatooine to make repairs.

# ANAKIN SKYWALKER

Desert Racer

**Anakin Skywalker** is a young boy who lives on the desert planet of Tatooine.

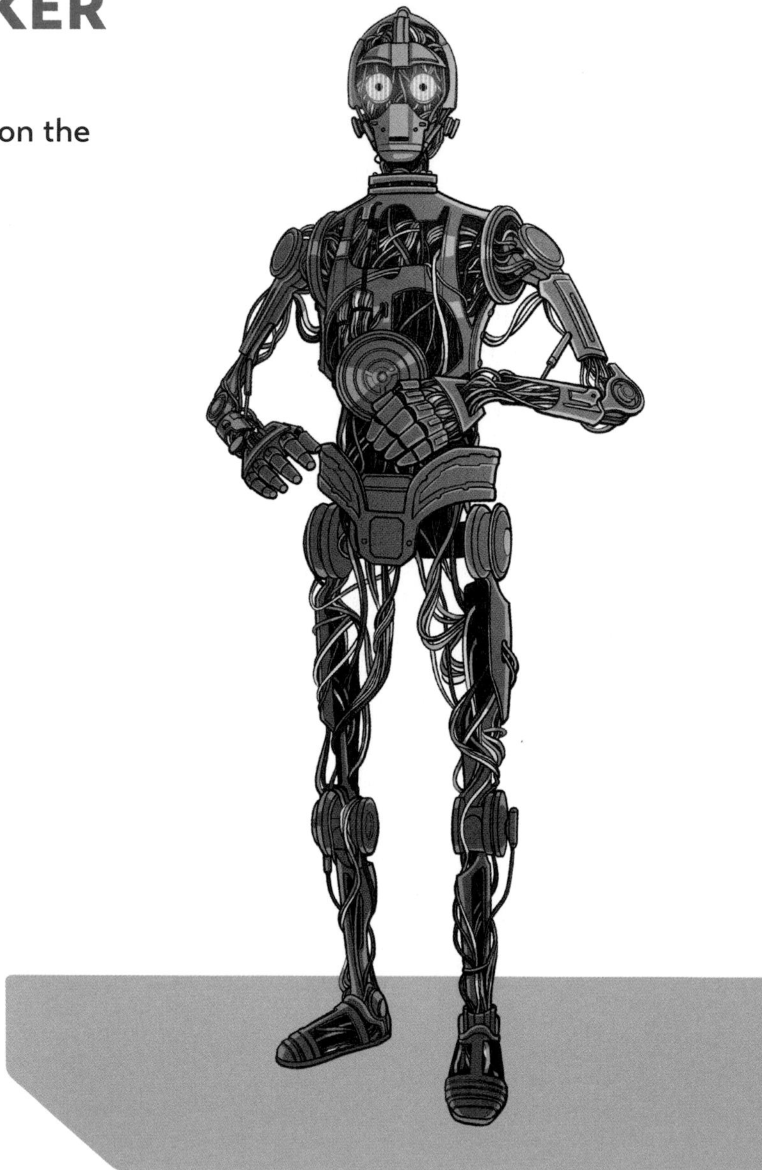

# C-3PO

Protocol Droid

**C-3PO** is a protocol droid that Anakin built to help his mother with chores around their home.

# WATTO

Junk Dealer

**Watto** is an alien who fixes ships on Tatooine. Anakin Skywalker works for Watto. Qui-Gon Jinn hopes Watto will help him repair their damaged ship so they can continue their mission to protect the queen and stop the Trade Federation. But Watto will not help them.

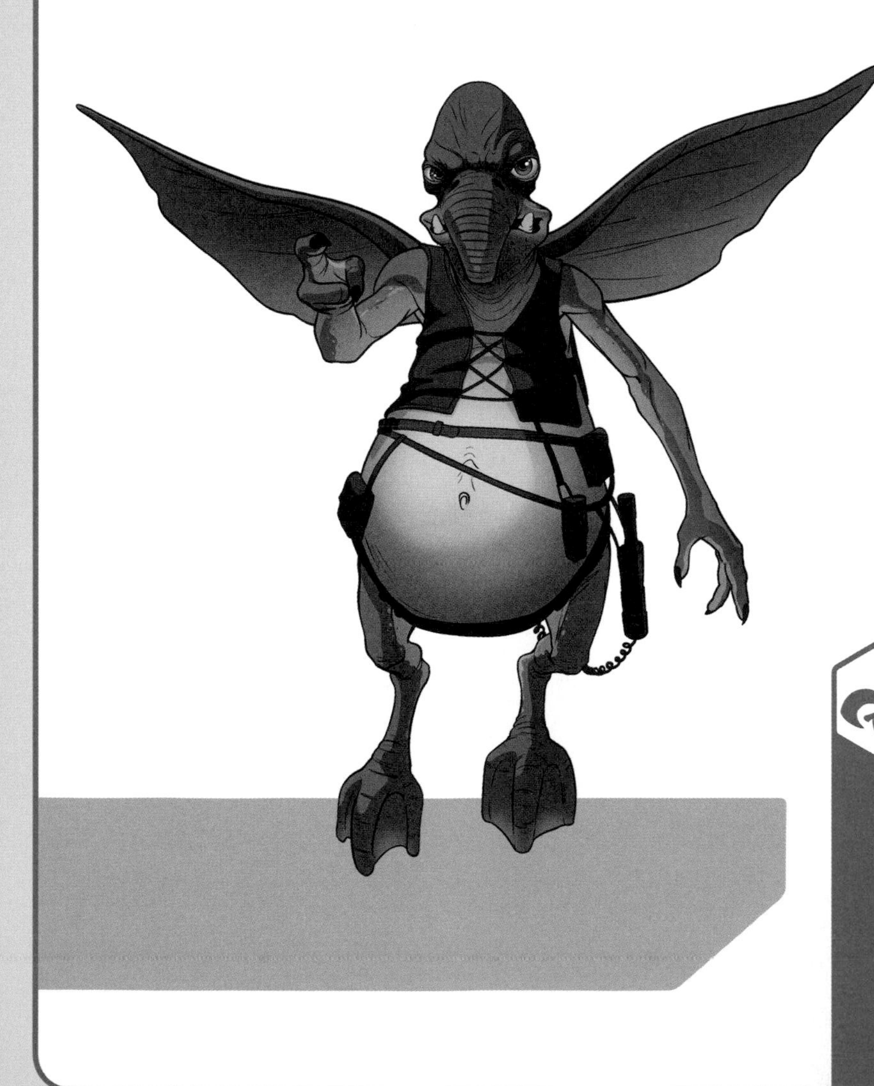

# PADMÉ

Queen in Disguise

**Padmé** is actually Queen Amidala, but she pretends she is one of the queen's handmaids to tag along to Watto's with Qui-Gon Jinn. Padmé and Anakin Skywalker become friends.

Anakin Skywalker knows how he can help Qui-Gon Jinn and Padmé get off of Tatooine. He competes in a podrace and wins! Anakin gives the money he wins from the race to Qui-Gon Jinn so he can fix his ship and continue his mission. Qui-Gon Jinn thinks Anakin Skywalker could be a Jedi and wants Anakin to come with him.

## SHMI SKYWALKER

Desert Dweller

**Shmi Skywalker** is Anakin's mother. Anakin does not want to leave his mom, but he does want to become a Jedi. Anakin decides to go with Qui-Gon Jinn, Obi-Wan Kenobi, Padmé, and R2-D2 back to the galaxy's capital, Coruscant.

## YODA

Grand Master of the Jedi Council

**Yoda** is a Jedi Master and the leader of the Jedi Council. He thinks Anakin is too old to learn how to become a Jedi. Yoda is more concerned about Naboo. When Padmé convinces the Gungans to help fight the Trade Federation after all, the Jedi decide to join the battle to save Naboo.

# SENATOR PALPATINE

Galactic Senator

**Senator Palpatine** is a senator and a friend of Queen Amidala's. Palpatine becomes the leader of the Galactic Senate, but he is secretly the evil Sith Lord, Darth Sidious, giving orders to the Trade Federation officials!

# DARTH MAUL

Sith Apprentice

**Darth Maul** is Darth Sidious's Sith apprentice. Darth Maul is a dangerous warrior who wields a double-bladed red lightsaber.

Darth Sidious sends Darth Maul to stop Qui-Gon Jinn and Obi-Wan Kenobi from rescuing Naboo from the Trade Federation. Darth Maul defeats Qui-Gon Jinn, but Obi-Wan Kenobi defeats Darth Maul.

Anakin Skywalker wants to help defeat the Trade Federation, too! He hops in a starfighter with R2-D2 and destroys the battleship that was controlling the droid army on Naboo. Queen Amidala and her people are finally free! And Obi-Wan convinces Yoda to let him train Anakin as a Padawan learner. Anakin Skywalker will become a Jedi, after all!

# STAR WARS™

## ATTACK OF THE CLONES

# PADMÉ AMIDALA

Galactic Senator

**Padmé Amidala** used to be the queen of Naboo. Now she is a senator for the planet, and someone is trying to hurt her!

# OBI-WAN KENOBI

Jedi Knight

**Obi-Wan Kenobi** is a Jedi Knight.

# ANAKIN SKYWALKER

Jedi Padawan

**Anakin Skywalker** is a Jedi in training. The Jedi Council sends Obi-Wan Kenobi and Anakin Skywalker to protect Padmé.

# ZAM WESELL

Bounty Hunter

**Zam Wesell** is a bounty hunter who is trying to hurt Padmé!

Obi-Wan Kenobi and Anakin Skywalker chase Zam Wesell to learn who sent her to hurt Padmé, but before they can find out, a poisonous dart hits Zam. Obi-Wan Kenobi decides to track down where the dart came from.

# CHANCELLOR PALPATINE

Leader of the Galactic Senate

**Chancellor Palpatine** is the leader of the Galactic Senate, but he is also secretly the evil Sith Lord Darth Sidious, who is trying to take over the galaxy. Palpatine orders Anakin Skywalker to stay with Padmé to protect her while Obi-Wan is away.

# R2-D2

Astromech Droid

**R2-D2** stays with Anakin and Padmé, too. The more time Anakin and Padmé spend together, the more they like each other. Pretty soon, they fall in love.

# KAMINOANS
Aliens

**Kaminoans** are strange aliens who live on a water planet called Kamino. Obi-Wan tracks the dart that hit Zam back to Kamino and discovers that someone from the Jedi Council has ordered the Kaminoans to create an army of clones!

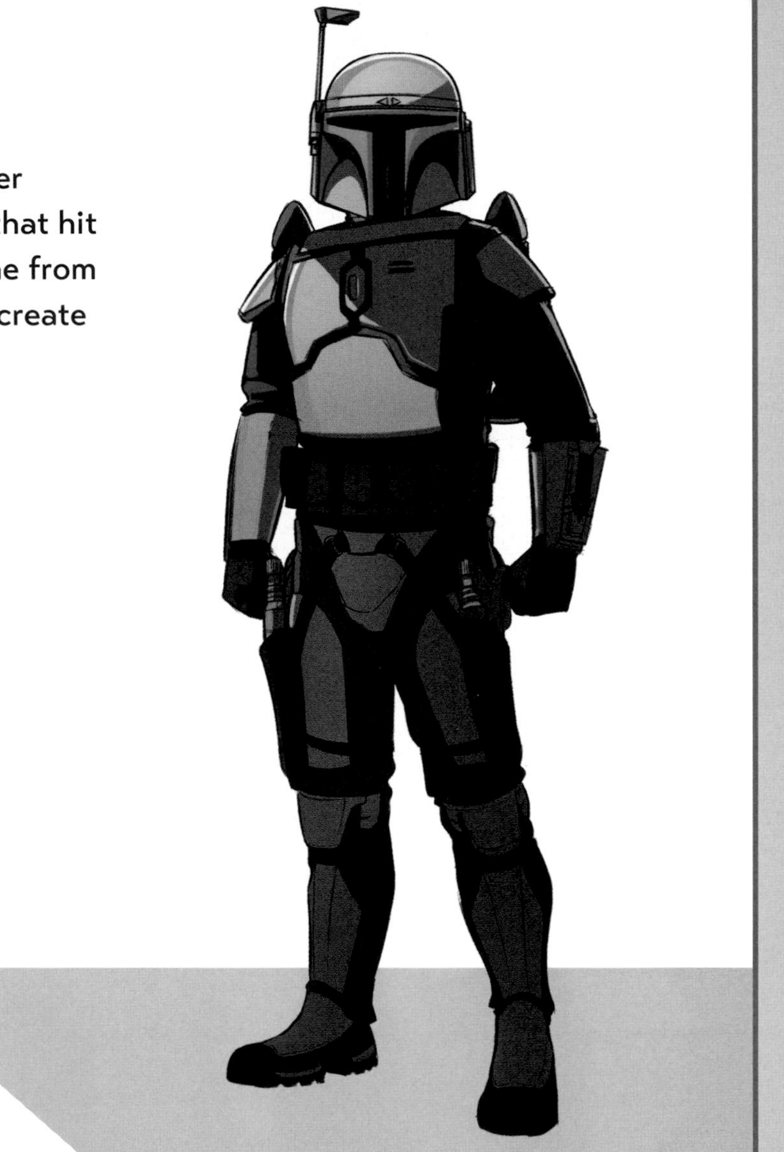

# JANGO FETT
Bounty Hunter

**Jango Fett** is a bounty hunter living on Kamino. The dart belonged to him! He is the one who sent Zam to hurt Padmé!

Obi-Wan Kenobi follows Jango Fett in his spaceship to the planet Geonosis. Obi-Wan Kenobi wants to find out who Jango Fett is working for.

# COUNT DOOKU

Sith Lord

**Count Dooku** is who Jango Fett is working for! Count Dooku is a former Jedi and the leader of an evil group called the Separatists, under the direction of Darth Sidious. They have plans to build a dangerous superweapon called the Death Star. Count Dooku captures Obi-Wan Kenobi, Padmé, and Anakin and forces them to fight dangerous beasts in an arena.

# ARENA BEASTS

Creatures

An **acklay**, a **nexu**, and a **reek** attack Obi-Wan, Anakin, and Padmé in the arena.

The three friends outsmart the beasts!

## MACE WINDU
Jedi Master

**Mace Windu** is a Jedi Master who arrives on Geonosis along with the rest of the Jedi to help Obi-Wan, Anakin, and Padmé. Mace Windu defeats Jango Fett!

## YODA
Grand Master of the Jedi Council

**Yoda** is a powerful Jedi Master and the leader of the Jedi Council, who also arrives on Geonosis to help. He brings the clone army from Kamino.

The Clone War has begun. The clone army fights the Separatists to maintain peace in the galaxy. Count Dooku escapes with the secret Death Star plans, but Obi-Wan, Anakin, Padmé, Yoda, and Mace Windu will not rest until they find him and put an end to the war.

In the midst of the battles, there is a moment of peace. Padmé and Anakin decide to get married in secret. Even though the galaxy is at war, there is still hope.

# STAR WARS™

## REVENGE OF THE SITH

# ANAKIN SKYWALKER

Jedi Knight

**Anakin Skywalker** is a talented Jedi Knight.

# OBI-WAN KENOBI

Jedi Master

**Obi-Wan Kenobi** is a wise Jedi Master.

The Jedi Council's clone army is at war with an evil group called the Separatists, who are trying to take over the galaxy. Anakin and Obi-Wan are on a mission for the Jedi Council. They fly their starships through a busy space battle.

# CHANCELLOR PALPATINE

Leader of the Galactic Senate

**Chancellor Palpatine** is the leader of the Galactic Senate, but he is also secretly the Sith Lord Darth Sidious, who is the leader of the Separatists.



# COUNT DOOKU

Sith Lord

**Count Dooku** is a former Jedi and a Separatist leader working with Darth Sidious to take control of the galaxy. Count Dooku has pretended to kidnap Palpatine to lure the Jedi into a trap.

Anakin and Obi-Wan arrive to rescue Palpatine. They battle Count Dooku with their lightsabers. Dooku is strong, but Anakin is stronger, and he soon defeats the Count. Palpatine pretends to be relieved, but he secretly starts to plot how to turn Anakin to the dark side of the Force so, as Darth Sidious, he can use Anakin's powers for evil.

# PADMÉ AMIDALA
Senator

**Padmé Amidala** is a senator for the planet Naboo. She is also secretly Anakin's wife. When Anakin returns from his mission to rescue Palpatine, Padmé tells him that she is pregnant. Anakin and Padmé are going to have a baby!

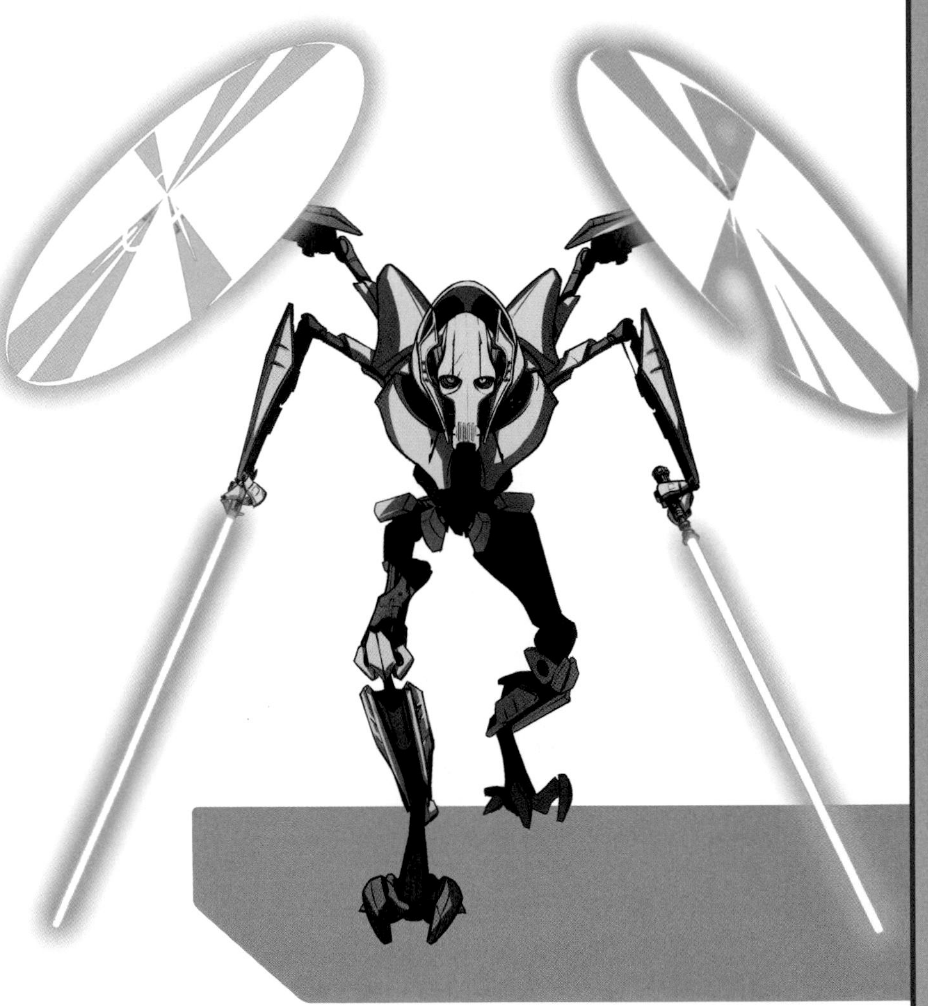

# GENERAL GRIEVOUS
Separatist Cyborg

**General Grievous** is a Separatist leader and a cyborg who was once organic but is now mostly machine. Grievous flees to the planet Utapau after Dooku's defeat.

Obi-Wan travels to Utapau with the Jedi Council's clone army to defeat General Grievous. Grievous is not a Jedi, but he uses four lightsabers that he stole from past duels. Obi-Wan is strong in the Force and he soon defeats the cyborg.

# DARTH SIDIOUS

Sith Lord

**Darth Sidious** is Chancellor Palpatine in disguise. An evil Sith Lord, he's also the leader of the Separatists and hopes to rule the galaxy. Darth Sidious reveals himself to Anakin and tries to convince him to join the dark side of the Force. Darth Sidious promises that he can teach Anakin how to protect Padmé and their future child.

# MACE WINDU

Jedi Master

**Mace Windu** is a Jedi Master. When Anakin learns that Chancellor Palpatine is really Darth Sidious, he warns Mace Windu.

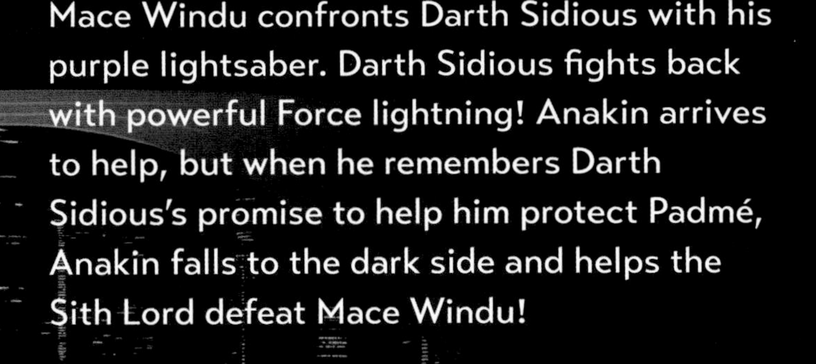

Mace Windu confronts Darth Sidious with his purple lightsaber. Darth Sidious fights back with powerful Force lightning! Anakin arrives to help, but when he remembers Darth Sidious's promise to help him protect Padmé, Anakin falls to the dark side and helps the Sith Lord defeat Mace Windu!

# CLONE TROOPERS

## Republic Soldiers

**Clone troopers** make up the Grand Army of the Republic. But Darth Sidious takes control of the army and orders them to defeat the Jedi instead!

# YODA

## Grand Master of the Jedi Council

**Yoda** is a powerful Jedi Master who manages to escape the clone troopers, but he needs to defeat Darth Sidious!

Yoda confronts Darth Sidious with his green lightsaber. But Darth Sidious is too powerful, even for Yoda. The Jedi Master has no choice but to escape and go into hiding to protect what remains of the Jedi Order.

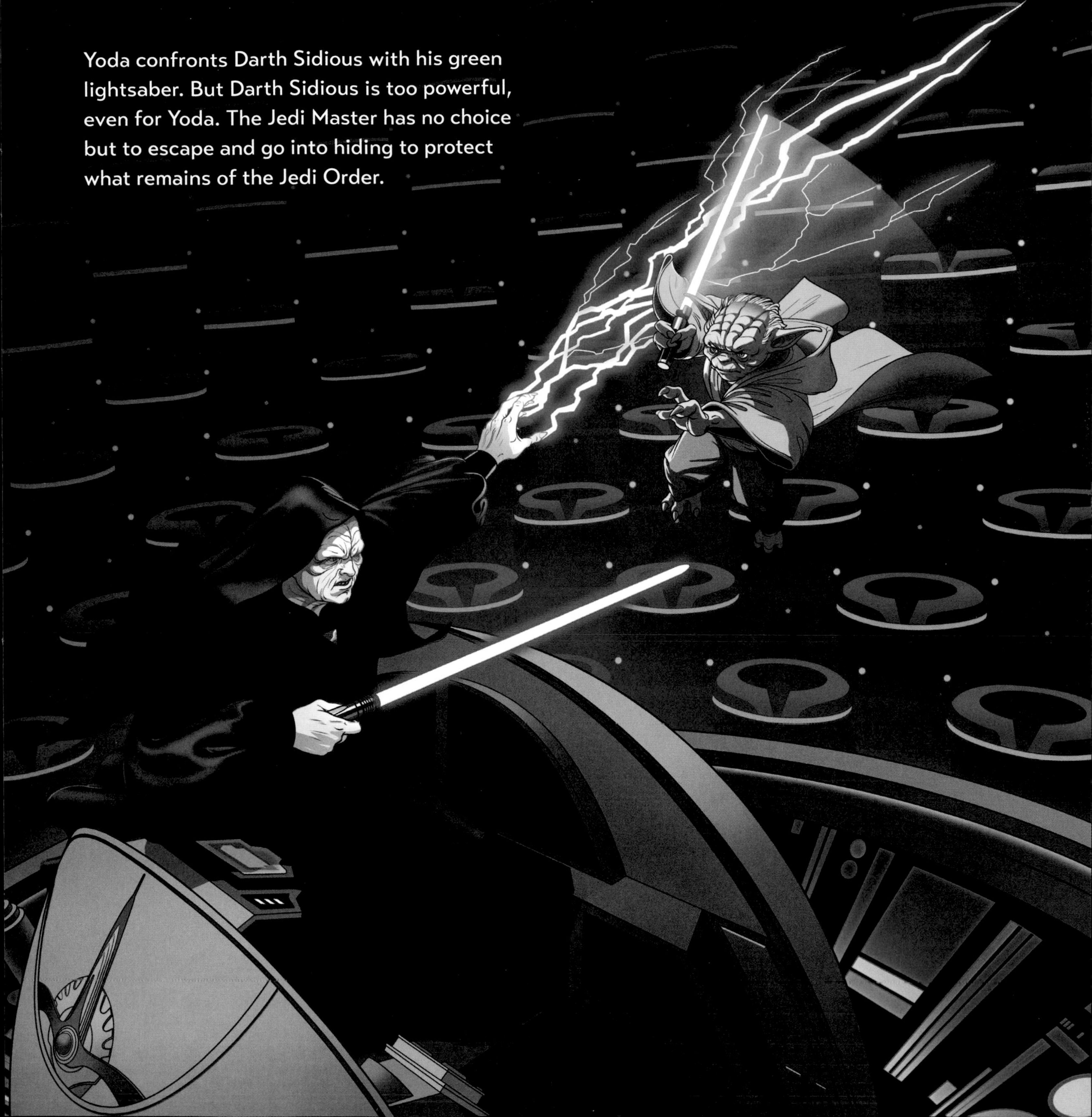

Obi-Wan also escapes from the clone troopers, and with Padmé's help, he follows Anakin to the fiery planet Mustafar. Obi-Wan wants to save Anakin from the dark side of the Force, but it is too late. Darth Sidous has turned Anakin's heart. Obi-Wan nearly defeats his former friend, and leaves Anakin on Mustafar, but Darth Sidious arrives to rescue Anakin. Darth Sidious gives Anakin a suit of black armor and a new Sith name . . .

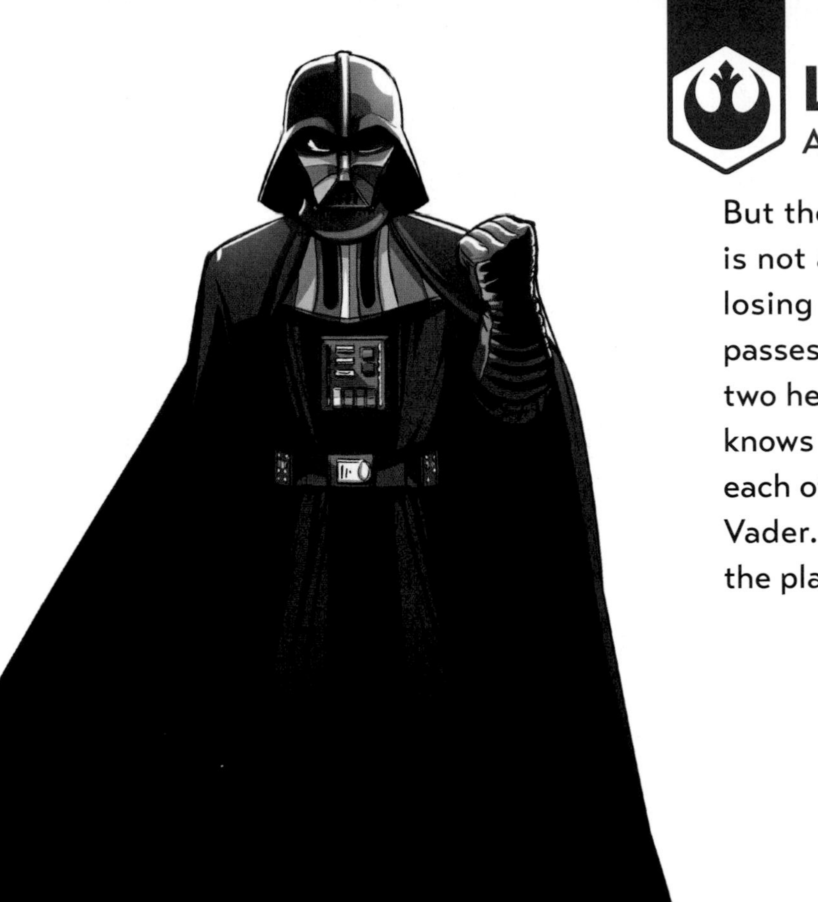

## LUKE & LEIA
Anakin Skywalker's Twin Children

But there is still hope. Even though Padmé is not able to survive the heartbreak of losing Anakin to the dark side, before she passes away she gives birth to not one but two healthy babies: **Luke** and **Leia.** Obi-Wan knows he needs to separate the babies from each other, to keep them safe from Darth Vader. Leia will grow up as a princess on the planet Alderaan . . .

## DARTH VADER
Sith Lord

**Darth Vader!** Anakin Skywalker is now a powerful Sith Lord who will use his powers for evil instead of good.

. . . while Luke will grow up with his aunt Beru and uncle Owen on his father's home planet Tatooine, under the distant but watchful eye of Obi-Wan Kenobi, who has decided to retreat into hiding there. Darth Sidious may have turned Anakin Skywalker to the dark side of the Force, but the Skywalker story is far from over.

# STAR WARS™

## A NEW HOPE

# LEIA ORGANA

Galactic Senator

**Leia Organa** is a princess and a senator for her home planet, Alderaan. Leia is also part of the Rebellion, a group of heroes fighting to defeat the evil Galactic Empire that has taken control of the galaxy.

# R2-D2

Astromech Droid

**R2-D2** is a faithful astromech droid in the Rebellion and is on board Leia's ship.

Leia has just received plans for the Empire's superweapon, the dreaded Death Star, from a group of brave rebel spies. But the Empire is chasing Leia's ship, so she gives the plans to R2-D2 and tells him to escape!

# C-3PO

Protocol Droid

**C-3PO** is an anxious protocol droid. He follows R2-D2 into an escape pod, and the two droids blast into space and land on the desert planet Tatooine.

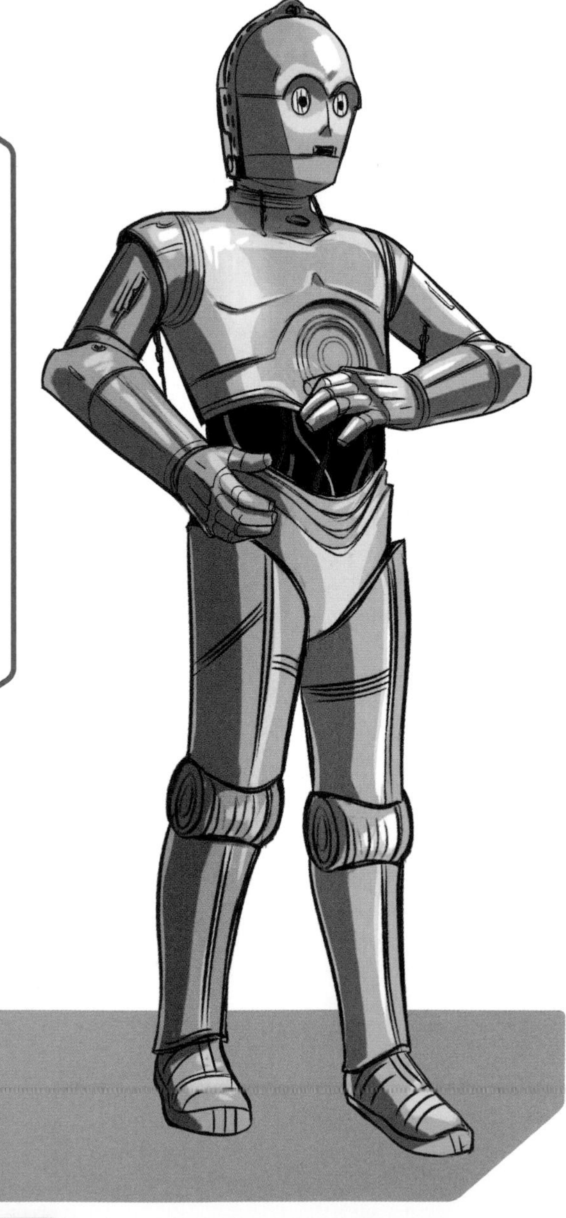

# JAWAS

Desert Scavengers

**Jawas** are little alien scavengers who live on Tatooine. They capture R2-D2 and C-3PO to sell them.

## UNCLE OWEN & AUNT BERU

Moisture Farmers

**Uncle Owen** and **Aunt Beru** are moisture farmers on Tatooine. Uncle Owen buys R2-D2 and C-3PO from the Jawas.

## LUKE SKYWALKER

Farm Boy

**Luke Skywalker** is Uncle Owen's nephew. He is tired of life on the farm and longs for adventure.

As Luke cleans the droids, R2-D2 accidentally plays part of a hologram message of Princess Leia asking for help from a man named Obi-Wan Kenobi. Luke is confused. Later, when R2-D2 rolls away to find Obi-Wan, Luke and C-3PO go after him, but they're soon attacked by Tusken Raiders!

## OBI-WAN KENOBI

Jedi Master

**Obi-Wan Kenobi** is an old Jedi Master also known as Ben. Fortunately, Obi-Wan arrives and scares the Tusken Raiders away. Obi-Wan explains that he knew Luke's father, who was also a Jedi but was defeated by the evil Sith Lord Darth Vader. Obi-Wan gives Luke his father's Jedi weapon, a lightsaber.



## TUSKEN RAIDERS

Fierce Nomads

**Tusken Raiders** are also known as Sand People. They live in the desert of Tatooine and ride big furry banthas. Banthas are gentle, but Tusken Raiders are not!

Luke decides to join Obi-Wan on his mission for Princess Leia so he can learn the ways of the Jedi like his father. But Luke, Obi-Wan, and the droids need a ship to leave Tatooine. So they go to a lively cantina to find a pilot. Luke almost gets into trouble, but Obi-Wan uses his lightsaber to protect the boy.

## GREEDO
Bounty Hunter

**Greedo** is a bounty hunter who is looking for Han Solo because Han owes money to a giant gangster named Jabba the Hutt. But Han manages to defeat Greedo and flies away from Tatooine in the *Falcon* with Obi-Wan, Luke, and the droids.

## HAN SOLO
Smuggler and Pilot

**Han Solo** is the pilot of the fastest ship in the galaxy, the *Millennium Falcon*. Han agrees to help Obi-Wan, Luke, and the droids get off Tatooine, for the right price.

Obi-Wan has Han take them to Princess Leia's home planet, Alderaan. But when they arrive, they realize the planet has been destroyed by the Empire's superweapon, the Death Star! The floating space station latches on to the *Falcon* with its tractor beam and pulls the ship inside.

## CHEWBACCA

*Millennium Falcon* Copilot

**Chewbacca**, also known as Chewie, is a furry Wookiee and Han's copilot. When Luke realizes that Princess Leia is imprisoned on the Death Star, he convinces Han and Chewie to pretend to escort the Wookiee as a prisoner through the space station so they can rescue the princess.

## STORMTROOPERS

Imperial Soldiers

**Stormtroopers** are soldiers for the Galactic Empire. A few stomtroopers climb on board the *Falcon*, but Han and Luke knock them out and put on their armor as a disguise. Meanwhile, Obi-Wan sneaks through the Death Star to turn off the space station's tractor beam so they can escape.

Luke, Han, and Chewie find Leia, but they soon get stuck in a stinky trash compactor. There's a scary swamp monster living under the garbage, and the walls suddenly start closing in on them! Luke contacts R2-D2 and C-3PO, who stop the walls from closing in, rescuing them just in time!

## GRAND MOFF TARKIN

Death Star Commander

**Grand Moff Tarkin** is the Imperial officer in charge of the Death Star. Both Tarkin and Vader report to the Galactic Empire's leader, the evil Emperor Palpatine.

## DARTH VADER

Sith Lord

**Darth Vader** is a warrior for the Galactic Empire and a powerful Sith Lord. Before turning to the dark side, Darth Vader was a promising Jedi Knight named Anakin Skywalker, who trained under Obi-Wan Kenobi.

Obi-Wan successfully turns off the tractor beam, but as he returns to the *Falcon*, he comes face to face with Darth Vader! The two former friends battle each other with their lightsabers. Obi-Wan distracts Darth Vader long enough for the heroes to sneak back on board the *Falcon* and escape. Then Obi-Wan allows Darth Vader to defeat him and becomes one with the Force.

With the plans for the Death Star, the Rebellion is able to find a weakness in the space station's design. Han, Chewie, and Luke fly into battle with other rebel pilots, and Luke uses the Force to fire a blast from his X-wing ship into the space station's weak point. Darth Vader manages to escape, but the Death Star explodes in a shower of sparks!

Thanks to Luke, Han, Chewie, Leia, and the droids, the Rebellion lives to continue the fight against Darth Vader and the evil Empire!

# STAR WARS™

## THE EMPIRE STRIKES BACK

# IMPERIAL PROBE DROID

Droid

An **Imperial probe droid** floats down to the icy planet Hoth. The Rebellion has built a secret base on the planet, but Darth Vader of the evil Empire has sent probe droids to the far reaches of the galaxy to discover their location.

# LUKE SKYWALKER

Rebel Hero and Jedi in Training

**Luke Skywalker** is a hero of the Rebellion and is learning the ways of the Jedi. He scouts the snowy plains of Hoth on his tauntaun looking for signs of the Empire.

A ferocious wampa attacks Luke and drags him back to its cave. Luke uses the Force to summon his lightsaber to free himself and defeat the wampa! Luke escapes the cave, but he's all alone and starts to freeze.

# OBI-WAN KENOBI

Jedi Master

**Obi-Wan Kenobi** is a Jedi Master and Luke's old friend. He appears to Luke through the Force. He tells Luke to go to a swamp planet called Dagobah to continue his Jedi training. But Luke first needs to be rescued from the snow.

# HAN SOLO

Rebel Captain

**Han Solo**, Luke's friend and fellow rebel hero, finds Luke just in time. Together they head back to the safety of the Rebellion's base.

Suddenly, the Empire arrives with a fleet of deadly, heavily armed walkers called AT-ATs! Rebel pilots and troops battle the walkers, but the Empire is too strong. They have to evacuate the base and fly to safety.

# LEIA ORGANA

Rebel Leader

**Leia Organa**, a leader of the Rebellion, wants to stay behind to make sure all the rebel troops get off the planet safely. But Han Solo knows she is in too much danger, so he convinces her to evacuate on his ship, the *Millennium Falcon*.

# CHEWBACCA

*Millennium Falcon* Copilot

**Chewbacca** the Wookiee, also known as Chewie, is Han Solo's copilot and a rebel hero. Chewie helps fly the *Millennium Falcon* away from Hoth. But Imperial Star Destroyers and TIE fighters chase them, damaging the *Falcon*'s hyperdrive.

To escape from the Imperial ships, Han flies the *Falcon* into a cave on an asteroid. But it turns out to be the belly of a huge space slug! The *Falcon* flies out of the creature's mouth right before the ship gets eaten.

## R2-D2
Astromech Droid

**R2-D2**, Luke's faithful astromech droid, helps navigate the Jedi to the remote planet Dagobah as Obi-Wan instructed. But the planet is so swampy that Luke crashes his X-wing.

## YODA
Jedi Master

**Yoda**, a short, green Jedi Master, finds Luke and R2-D2 in the swamp. Yoda is very old and wise. He doesn't think Luke is patient enough to learn the ways of the Jedi. But Obi-Wan communicates with Yoda through the Force and convinces him to train Luke.

Meanwhile, the heroes in the *Millennium Falcon* need a safe place to land away from the Empire, where they can repair their ship. Han navigates them to the beautiful floating Cloud City above the planet Bespin.

# LANDO CALRISSIAN

Scoundrel

**Lando Calrissian** is an old friend of Han's. Lando is charming, and he runs Cloud City. He says he will help the heroes repair the *Falcon*, but Leia doesn't trust Lando.

# C-3PO

Protocol Droid

**C-3PO** is a faithful protocol droid for the Rebellion. Shortly after the heroes arrive in Cloud City, C-3PO is captured and dismantled for parts! Chewbacca finds C-3PO and works to put him back together.

Across the galaxy, Luke trains with Yoda in the swamp of Dagobah. Yoda tells Luke to connect with the Force and use it for knowledge and defense. But Luke senses that his friends are in danger. He insists on leaving Yoda and his training behind to help them.

# DARTH VADER

Sith Lord

**Darth Vader** is an evil Sith Lord and a leader of the Empire. Sensing Luke Skywalker's growing power in the Force, he arrives in Cloud City and forces Lando to hand over Han, Leia, Chewie, and C-3PO. Luke was right; his friends are in trouble. But Darth Vader is just using them to lure Luke into a trap!

# BOBA FETT

Bounty Hunter

**Boba Fett** is the clone son of Jango Fett and a bounty hunter who helped Darth Vader find the heroes. Boba Fett also works for a gangster named Jabba the Hutt. Han owes Jabba money, and Boba Fett plans to take Han to Jabba.

Han is going to be frozen in carbonite and taken to Jabba. Leia and Chewbacca are sad and angry. Leia loves Han.

Luke arrives in Cloud City and must face Darth Vader. The two duel with their lightsabers. Luke is strong, but Darth Vader is stronger. He tells Luke to join him in fighting for the Empire, but Luke refuses. He also tells Luke that he is Luke's father! Luke is shocked, but he manages to escape with Leia, Chewbacca, and the droids. The heroes will have to find a way to save Han, and defeat the Empire once and for all.

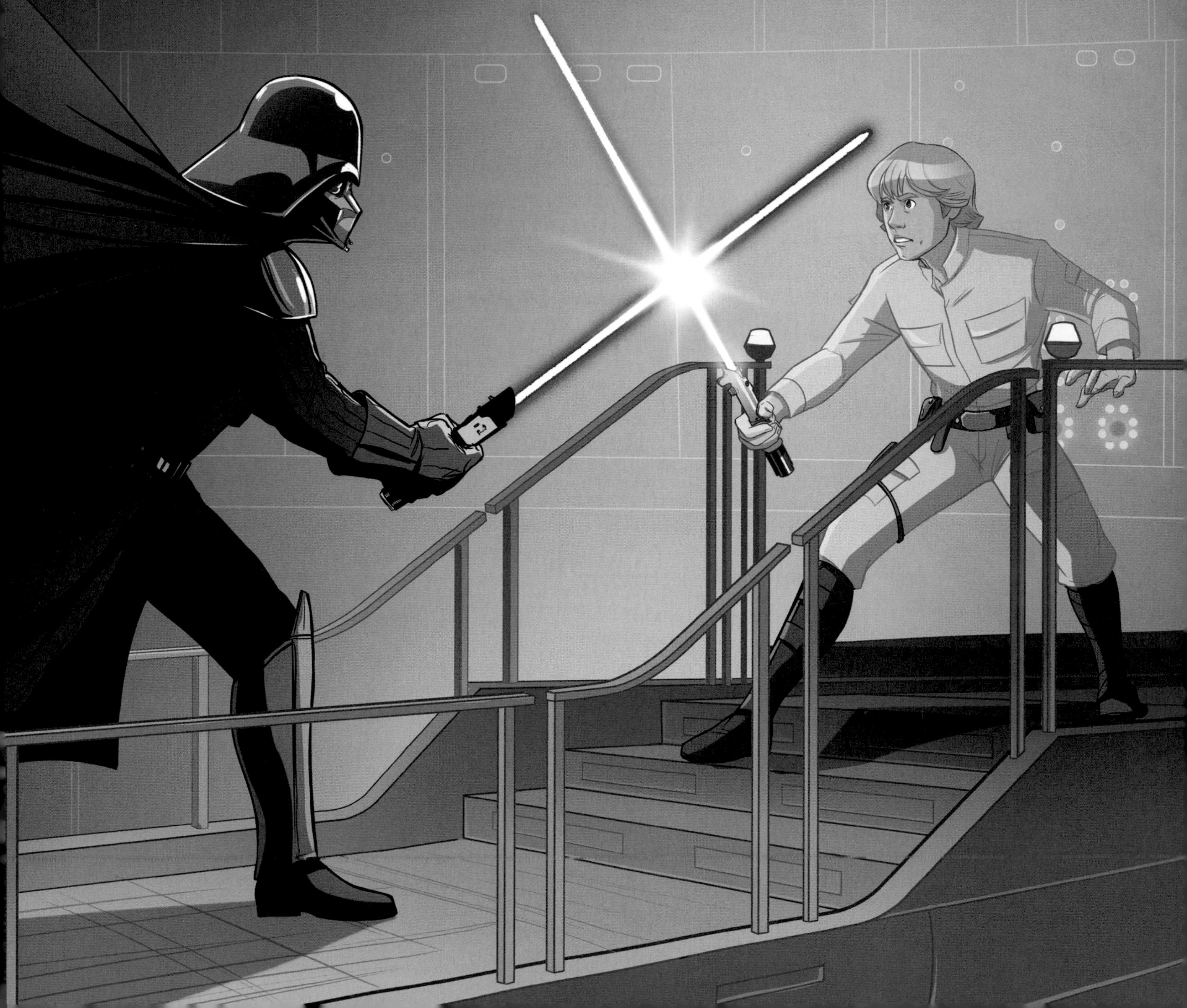

# STAR WARS™

## RETURN OF THE JEDI

## JABBA THE HUTT

Crime Lord

**Jabba the Hutt** is an evil gangster. He is big and slimy.

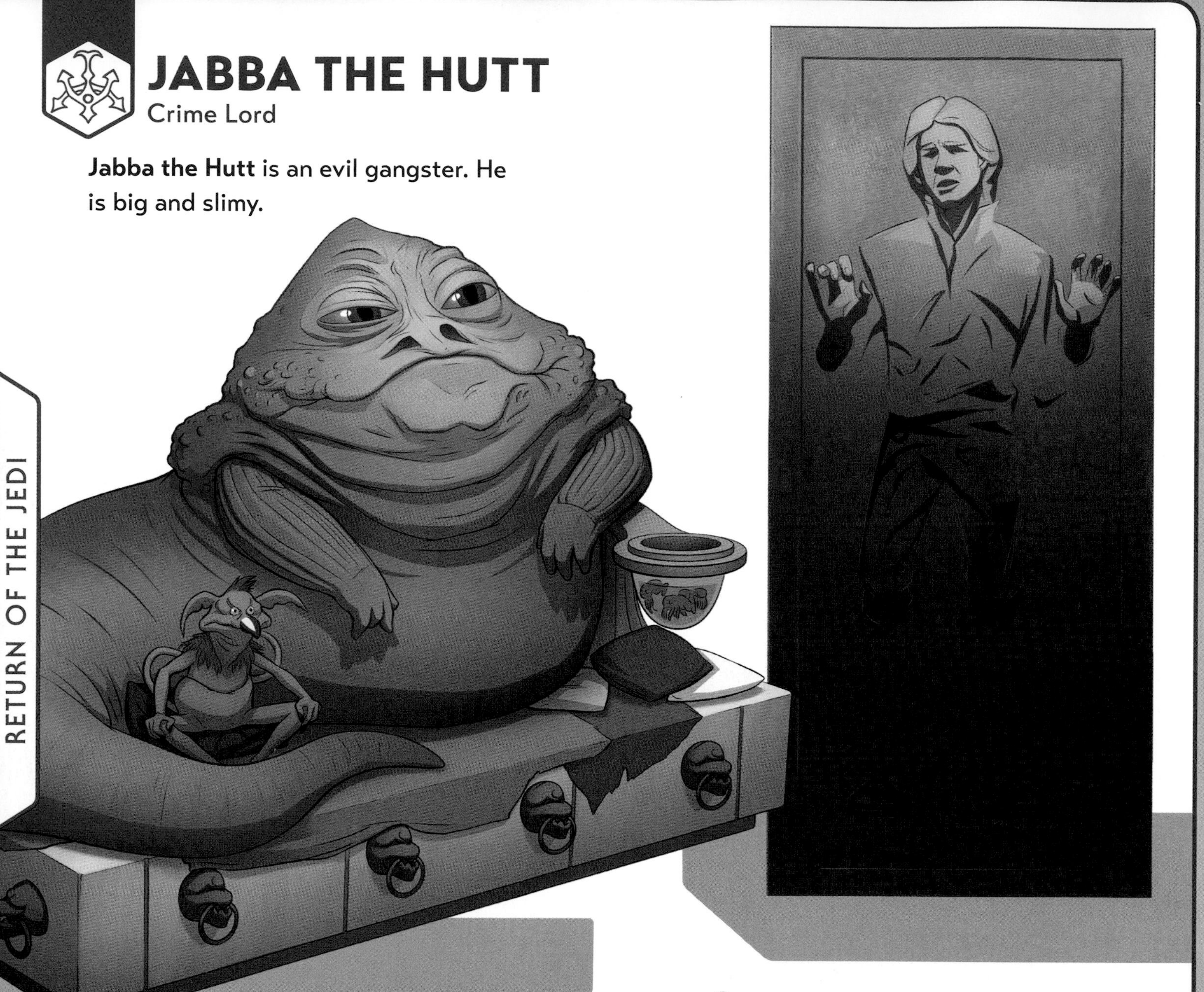

RETURN OF THE JEDI

## HAN SOLO

Rebel Captain

**Han Solo** is a rebel hero. He is trapped in carbonite at Jabba's palace on Tatooine.

## LEIA ORGANA

Rebel Leader

**Leia Organa** is a leader of the Rebellion. She disguises herself as a bounty hunter so they can enter Jabba's palace and rescue Han. Leia is able to release Han from the carbonite, but she is caught by Jabba.

## CHEWBACCA

*Millennium Falcon* Copilot

**Chewbacca** is a Wookiee and a friend of Han's.

# LUKE SKYWALKER

Jedi Knight

**Luke Skywalker** is a Jedi and a friend of Han, Chewbacca, and Leia's. He enters Jabba's palace and tells the gangster to free his friends. But Jabba opens a trapdoor under Luke instead, and the Jedi falls into a shadowy chamber!

# RANCOR

Deadly Beast

A **rancor** is a deadly beast with giant claws and sharp teeth. A rancor attacks Luke down in the chamber, but Luke is able to outsmart the beast and defeat it.

Jabba decides to feed his prisoners to a sand monster out in the desert called the Sarlacc.

## R2-D2

Astromech Droid

**R2-D2** is Luke's faithful astromech droid, and the two have a plan! Just as Luke is about to be fed to the Sarlacc, he uses the Force to leap up into the air, retrieve his lightsaber from R2, and take out Jabba's guards who were holding Han and Chewie prisoner.

## BOBA FETT

Bounty Hunter

**Boba Fett** is a fearsome bounty hunter who works for Jabba the Hutt. Boba Fett flies in on his jetpack to try to stop Luke, but Han knocks into him, causing Boba Fett to fall into the Sarlacc pit! In all the chaos, Leia manages to defeat Jabba the Hutt. The heroes are finally free!

## MON MOTHMA

Rebel Leader

**Mon Mothma** is one of the leaders of the Rebellion. The rebels need to destroy the Empire's new Death Star, a dangerous superweapon that is still under construction. A team of rebels will land on the nearby forest moon of Endor to deactivate the Death Star's protective shield generator so rebel pilots can fly in and destroy it.

## YODA

Jedi Master

**Yoda** is a wise Jedi Master. Luke travels to the swamp planet Dagobah to see Yoda, but the Jedi Master is very old and is growing weak. He tells Luke to confront Darth Vader—the evil Sith Lord and a leader of the Empire who is also Luke's father. Before passing away and becoming one with the Force, Yoda also tells Luke that there is another Skywalker: Leia. Leia is Luke's sister.

Luke, Leia, Han, and Chewie sneak down to Endor, but they are spotted by Imperial scout troopers on speeder bikes. Luke and Leia chase after the troopers through the forest and knock them off their speeder bikes! But Luke and Leia get separated from each other.

## C-3PO

Protocol Droid

**C-3PO** is a golden protocol droid faithful to the Rebellion. The Ewoks think that C-3PO is a god! To help convince them, Luke uses the Force to raise C-3PO up in the air in the throne the Ewoks made for him. C-3PO convinces the Ewoks to free his friends, then he tells them about the evil Empire. The Ewoks agree to help the rebels!



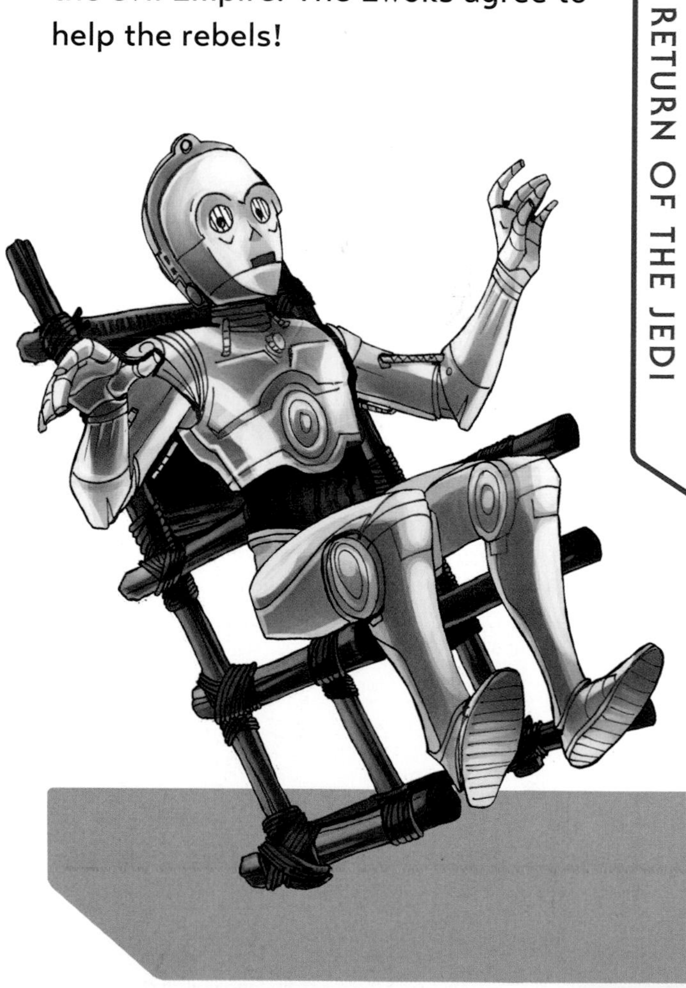

## WICKET

Ewok

**Wicket** is a little Ewok who lives on Endor. He finds Leia and befriends her. He takes Leia back to his treehouse village. Other Ewoks have captured Han, Chewie, and Luke and tied them up.

## DARTH VADER

Sith Lord

**Darth Vader** is a Sith Lord who was once a Jedi named Anakin Skywalker. He is also Luke Skywalker's father. Luke surrenders to Darth Vader. He believes there is still good in his father, and urges him to let go of his hate and leave the dark side. But Darth Vader says it is too late.

## DARTH SIDIOUS

Evil Emperor

**Darth Sidious** is Darth Vader's master and the Emperor, the leader of the Galactic Empire. Vader takes Luke to Darth Sidious, who is eager to have Luke join him as an apprentice. But Luke refuses to turn to the dark side.

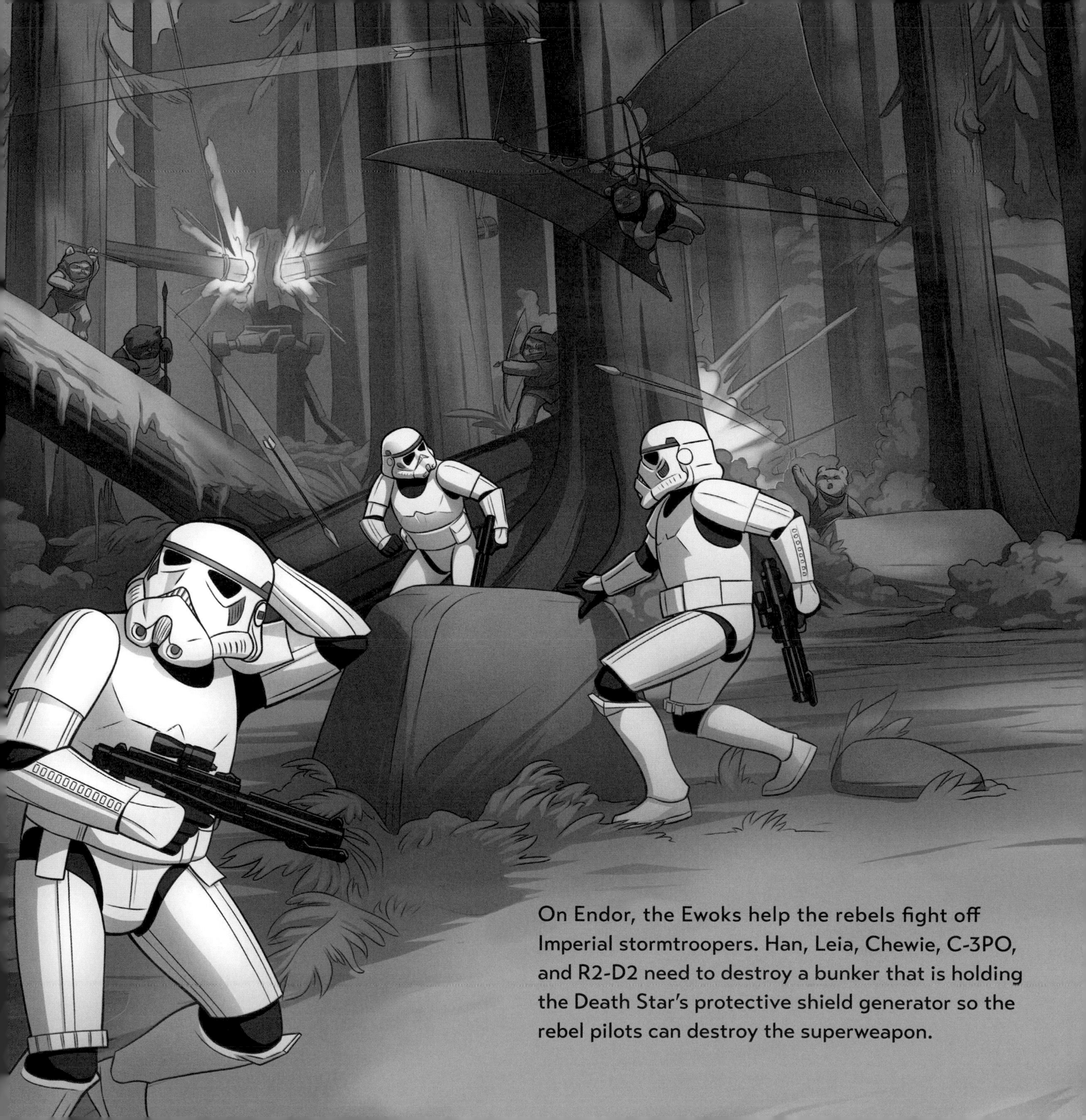

On Endor, the Ewoks help the rebels fight off Imperial stormtroopers. Han, Leia, Chewie, C-3PO, and R2-D2 need to destroy a bunker that is holding the Death Star's protective shield generator so the rebel pilots can destroy the superweapon.

# ADMIRAL ACKBAR

Rebel Commander

**Admiral Ackbar** is the commander leading the rebel pilots into battle in space. Their attack was supposed to be a surprise, but the admiral soon realizes that Imperial fighters are waiting for them!

# LANDO CALRISSIAN

Rebel Leader

**Lando Calrissian** is a friend of Han's who has joined the Rebellion. He is flying Han's ship, the *Millennium Falcon*, during the space battle. When Han and the rebels finally blow up the bunker on Endor, the Death Star's protective shield is deactived and Lando flies into the superweapon to destroy it.

On board the Death Star, Darth Sidious attacks Luke with powerful Force lightning. Suddenly, Darth Vader picks up Darth Sidious and throws him into the Death Star's reactor shaft, defeating him once and for all! Luke removes his father's mask to see the face of Anakin Skywalker. He was right. There is still good in his father. But in defeating Darth Sidious, Anakin has used all his power and energy, and soon he becomes one with the Force.

Luke escapes from the Death Star before the rebels blow it up. The Death Star explodes in a shower of sparks! Luke, Leia, Han, Chewie, Lando, R2-D2, C-3PO, and the rebels have done it. They have destroyed the Emperor and the Death Star, and in turn the Empire will soon be defeated. The galaxy will be free once more.

# STAR WARS™

## THE FORCE AWAKENS

## LOR SAN TEKKA

Explorer

**Lor San Tekka** is an old explorer who lives on the desert planet Jakku.

## POE DAMERON

Resistance Pilot

**Poe Dameron** is a pilot for the Resistance, a group fighting to stop the First Order, an evil army rising to power in the galaxy. Poe is on a mission for the Resistance to find Lor San Tekka and get information from him that could help defeat the First Order.

## BB-8

Astromech Droid

**BB-8** is Poe's faithful astromech droid. Poe gives BB-8 the information from Lor San Tekka and tells the droid to run away into the desert to make sure it doesn't end up in the wrong hands.

## KYLO REN

First Order Warrior

**Kylo Ren** is a First Order warrior trained in the dark side of the Force. He arrives on Jakku to find Lor San Tekka, as well.

## CAPTAIN PHASMA

Stormtrooper Commander

**Captain Phasma** is the cruel leader of the First Order's army of soldiers called stormtroopers. Captain Phasma's troopers have captured Poe Dameron on Jakku.

## FN-2187

Stormtrooper

**FN-2187** is one of the stormtroopers under Phasma's command. But FN-2187 doesn't want to fight for the First Order.

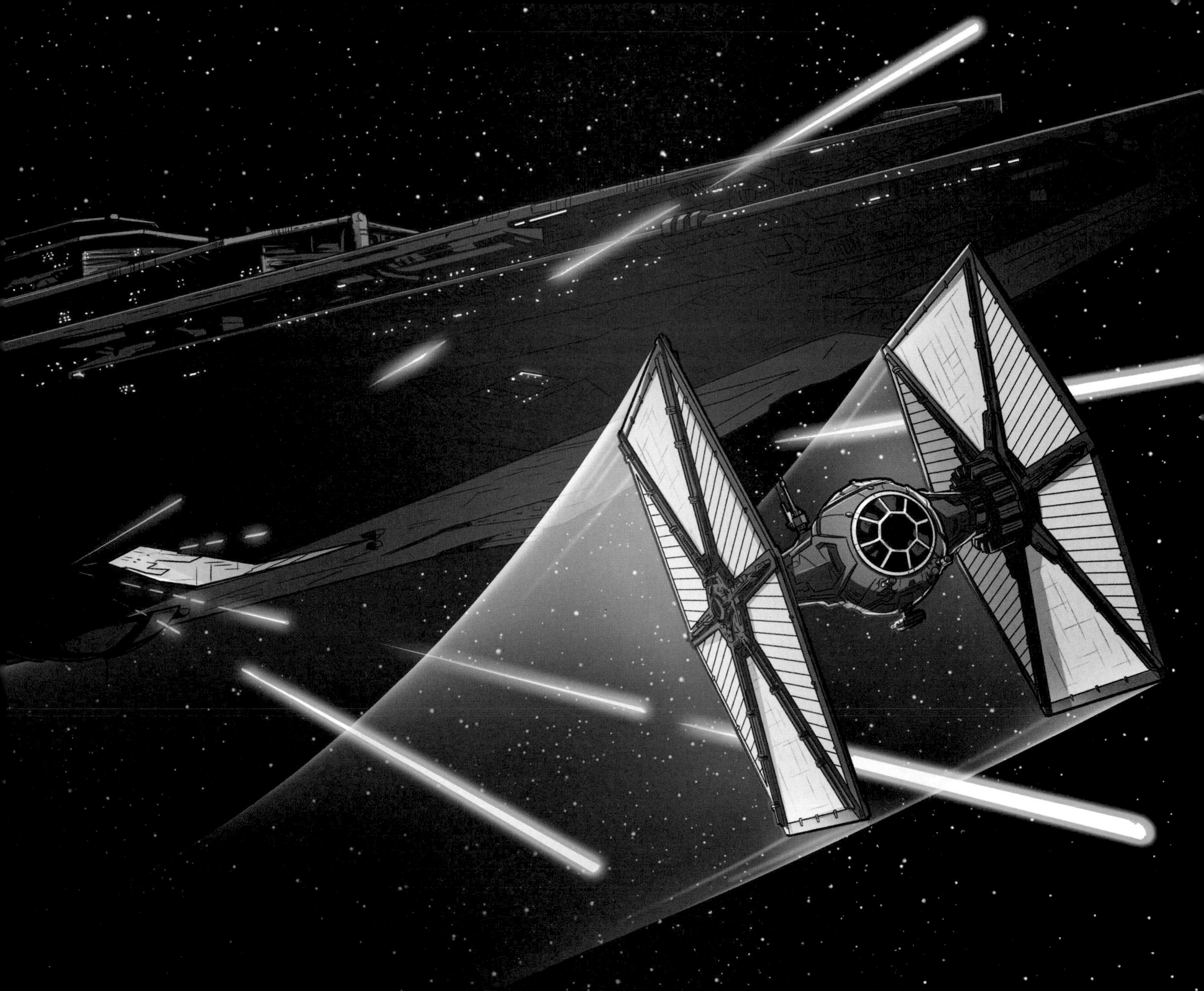

FN-2187 rescues Poe, and the two escape from a First Order Star Destroyer in a stolen TIE fighter. Poe calls FN-2817 "Finn" and tells him that they need to go back to Jakku to find BB-8. Suddenly, their TIE is struck by a blast from the First Order and they spiral down to the planet, crash-landing in the dunes.

# TEEDO
## Desert Scavenger

A **Teedo** is a desert scavenger. A Teedo riding a luggabeast on Jakku captures BB-8 in a net. BB-8 beeps for help!



# REY
## Desert Scavenger

**Rey** is a lonely desert scavenger living inside an old fallen AT-AT walker on Jakku. She hears BB-8's beeps and rescues the droid from the Teedo.

Finn survives the TIE fighter crash, but he can't find Poe. He wanders the desert of Jakku until he finds an outpost, where he runs into BB-8 and Rey. The three have to work together to escape when First Order stormtroopers and TIEs attack the outpost. They steel an old ship and blast off into space.

Rey and Finn decide to help BB-8 get back to the Resistance, but their ship is suddenly swallowed by a much bigger ship.

## CHEWBACCA
Copilot

**Chewbacca** the Wookiee is also a rebel hero and is Han's copilot. Han and Chewie are happy to have found their old ship, the *Millennium Falcon*. But two gangs suddenly show up demanding money from Han.



## HAN SOLO
Smuggler

**Han Solo** is the pilot of the cargo ship that captures Rey, Finn, and BB-8's ship. He is also an old war hero who once helped the Rebellion defeat the evil Galactic Empire.

In an attempt to help Han and Chewie escape from the two gangs, Rey accidentally opens compartments on the cargo ship that are holding deadly rathtars! Chaos erupts, but the heroes are able to escape in the *Millennium Falcon*. Han agrees to help them get BB-8 back to the Resistance.

# MAZ KANATA

Resistance Ally

**Maz Kanata** is a wise old alien and a friend of Han's. The *Millennium Falcon* arrives at Maz's castle on the lush planet Takodana. Maz wants to help Finn and Rey, and sensing Rey's connection with the Force, she gives the girl Luke Skywalker's lightsaber. But Rey is frightened by the Force that's awakening inside her.

# BAZINE NETAL

First Order Spy

**Bazine Netal** is a spy for the First Order inside Maz's castle. She alerts the First Order that Han, Chewie, Finn, Rey, and BB-8 are there.

The First Order attacks Maz's castle, but the Resistance flies in to fight, as well! The dark warrior Kylo Ren manages to capture Rey before the First Order escapes.

# GENERAL LEIA ORGANA

Resistance Leader

**General Leia Organa** is the wise leader of the Resistance who once helped lead the Rebellion to defeat the evil Galactic Empire. Leia and Han had a son together named Ben. But Ben became Kylo Ren when he turned to the dark side of the Force.

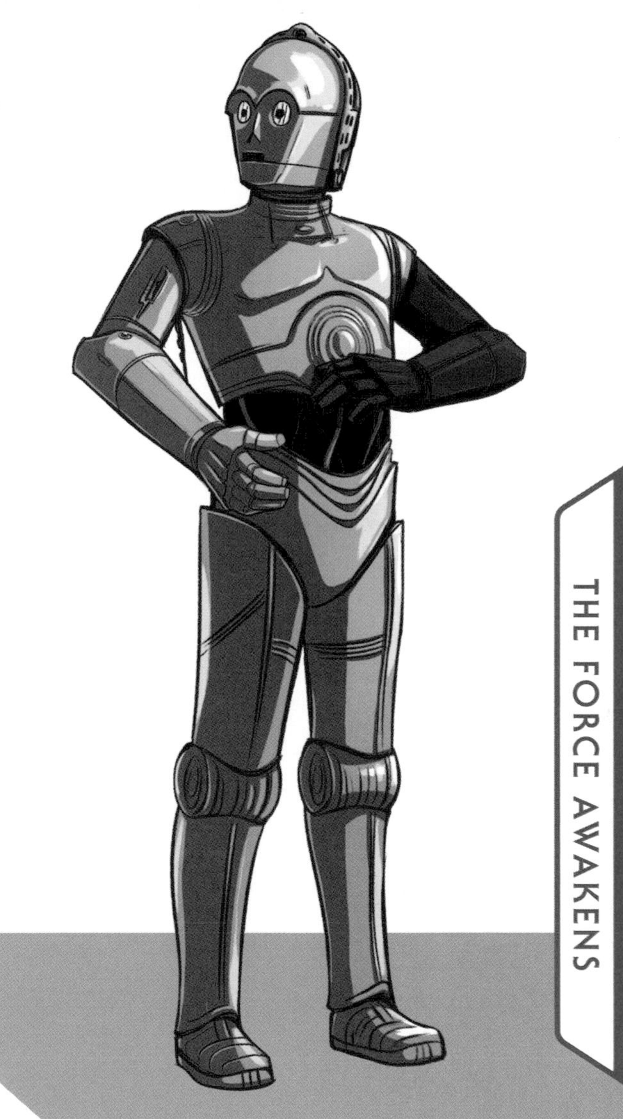

# C-3PO

Protocol Droid

**C-3PO** is an anxious protocol droid who serves alongside Leia and once had many adventures with Han and Chewie. C-3PO suspects that they might not recognize him now, though, since he has a new red arm.

# GENERAL HUX

First Order Officer

**General Hux** is a leader of the First Order. He has overseen the creation of the First Order superweapon, the Starkiller. Far more powerful than the Empire's Death Star, the Starkiller destroys an entire star system on Hux's command.

# SUPREME LEADER SNOKE

First Order Leader

**Supreme Leader Snoke** is the leader of the First Order and Kylo Ren's master in his training in the dark side of the Force. Leia and Han know that Snoke turned their son Ben's heart to make him Kylo Ren. And when Han sneaks onto the Starkiller Base to try to save his son, Kylo solidifies his loyalty to Snoke by defeating his own father.

Rey and Finn confront Kylo in the forest on Starkiller Base, but Kylo badly injures Finn with his glowing red lightsaber. Rey allows the Force to flow through her so she can battle Kylo with Luke Skywalker's blue lightsaber. Kylo is strong in the Force, but Rey is stronger. She injures Kylo and escapes from the base with Chewbacca and Finn on board the *Millennium Falcon*.

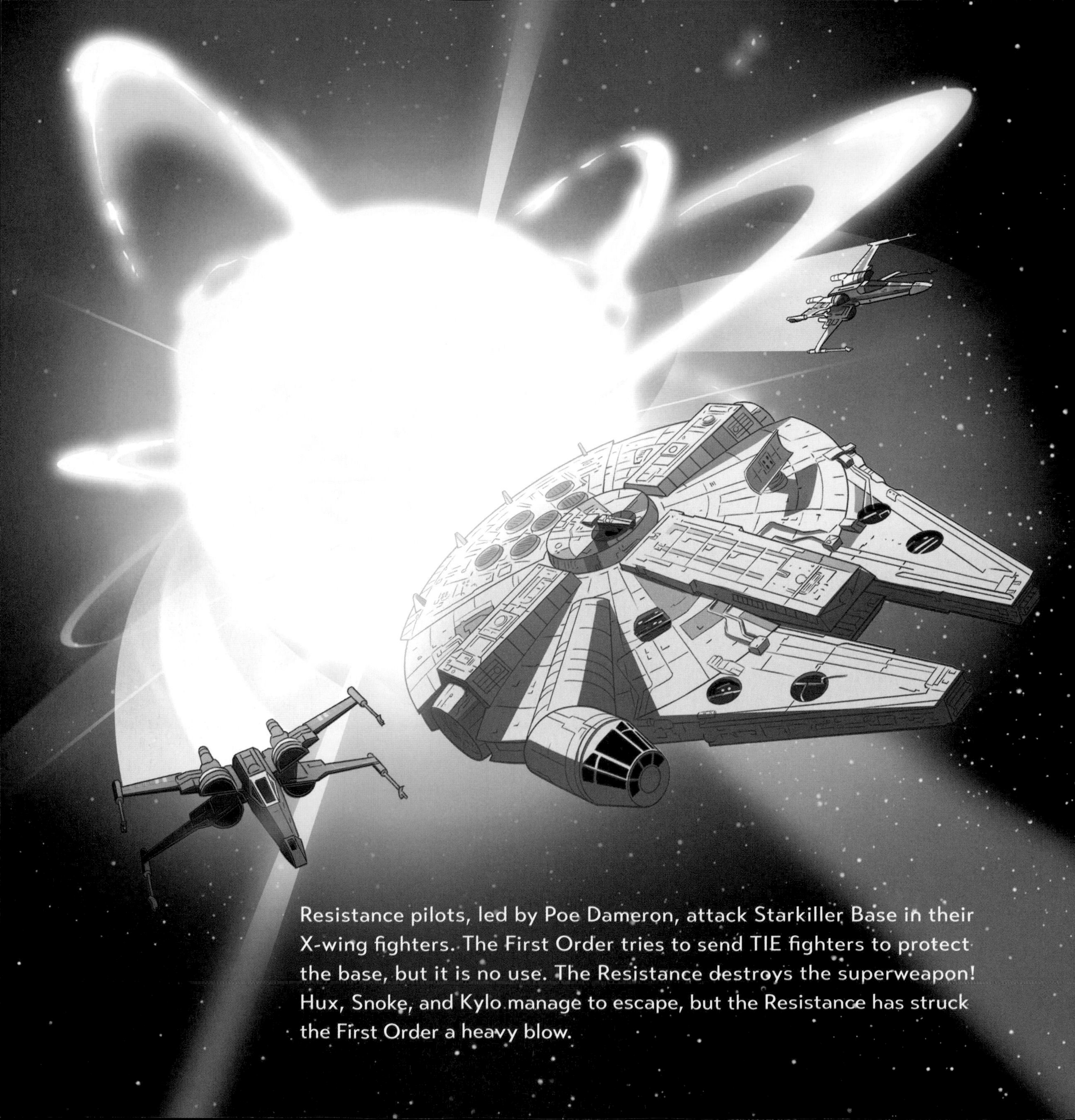

Resistance pilots, led by Poe Dameron, attack Starkiller Base in their X-wing fighters. The First Order tries to send TIE fighters to protect the base, but it is no use. The Resistance destroys the superweapon! Hux, Snoke, and Kylo manage to escape, but the Resistance has struck the First Order a heavy blow.

## R2-D2
Astromech Droid

**R2-D2** is Luke Skywalker's old astromech droid. When BB-8 shares the information that he got from Lor San Tekka, R2-D2 beeps awake. BB-8 has part of a map that leads to Luke Skywalker, and R2-D2 has the other part of the map!

## LUKE SKYWALKER
The Last Jedi

**Luke Skywalker** is Leia's brother and the last remaining Jedi in the galaxy. Leia sends Rey to find Luke. The Resistance needs Luke's help to defeat the First Order, and Rey needs help learning the ways of the Force.

Rey, Chewie, and R2-D2 set off in the *Millennium Falcon* to fly across the galaxy and find Luke Skywalker. He is their only hope!

# STAR WARS™

THE LAST JEDI

# POE DAMERON

Resistance Pilot

**Poe Dameron** is a Resistance pilot. The Resistance destroyed the First Order's superweapon, the Starkiller, but now the evil army has found the Resistance base and wants to destroy it.

# BB-8

Astromech Droid

**BB-8** is Poe's faithful astromech droid, who helps navigate Poe's X-wing fighter.

Poe leads Resistance A-wings, X-wings, and bombers into battle. They need to distract the First Order long enough to evacuate their base so the Resistance fleet can jump to the safety of hyperspace.

# GENERAL LEIA ORGANA

Resistance Leader

**General Leia Organa** is the leader of the Resistance, a group fighting to stop the First Order, an evil army rising to power in the galaxy. Her son, Ben, turned to the dark side and became . . .

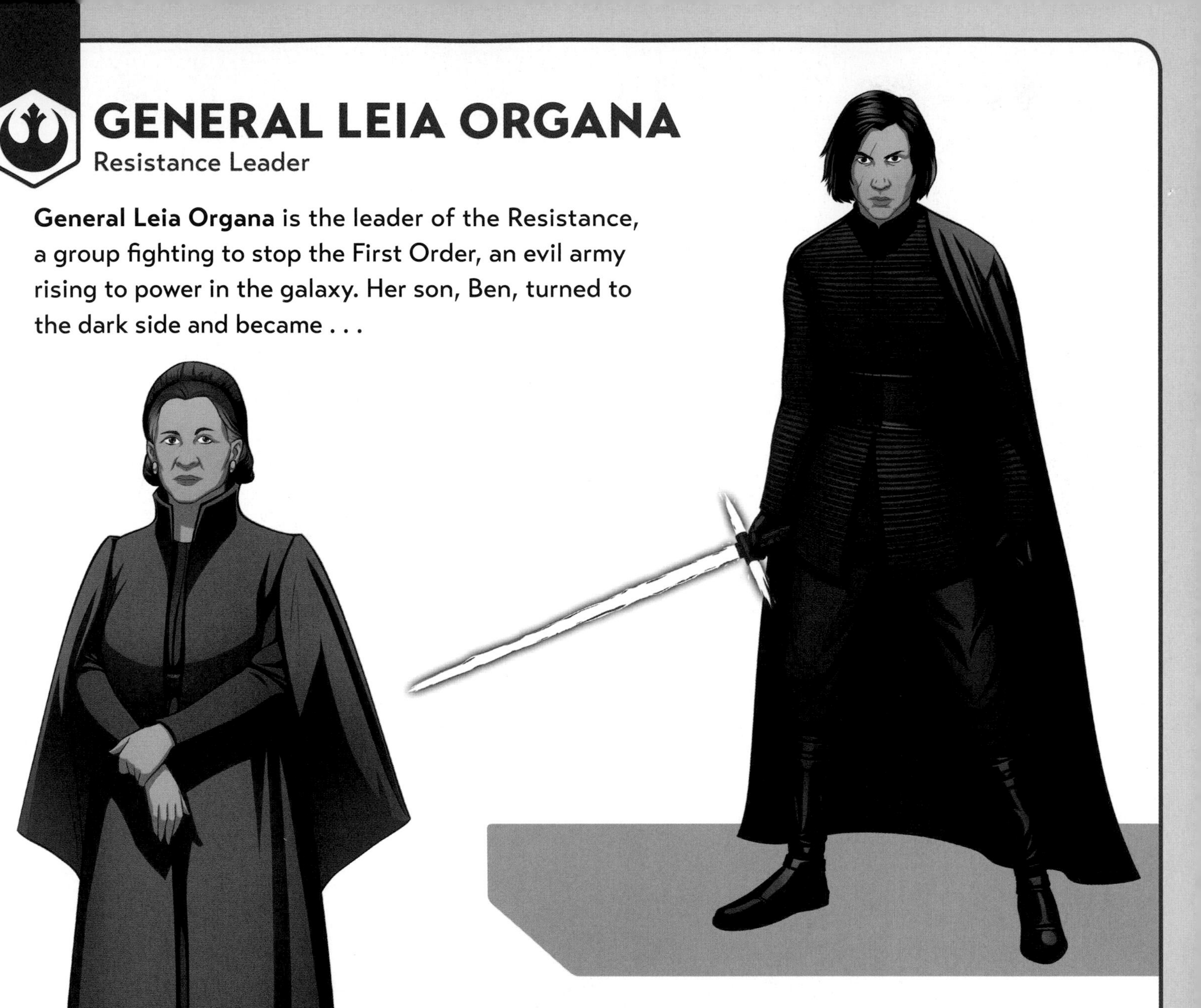

# KYLO REN

First Order Warrior

**Kylo Ren!** Kylo is a dark warrior for the First Order. He attacks the Resistance fleet in his TIE fighter alongside other First Order pilots.

The First Order attack damages the main Resistance ship, and Leia is sucked out into space! Leia, sensitive to the Force, uses it to pull herself back into the ship, but she is hurt and unable to lead. To make matters worse, the Resistance realizes that the First Order can track their ships through hyperspace.

# FINN

## Resistance Hero

**Finn** is a former First Order stormtrooper and a new Resistance hero. Finn is worried about the First Order catching him, though, and tries to leave the Resistance, but he's stopped by . . .

# ROSE TICO

## Resistance Mechanic

**Rose Tico!** Rose is a mechanic for the Resistance. Finn and Rose come up with a plan to deactivate the First Order's tracking device so the Resistance ships can safely jump to hyperspace without being followed.

Finn, Rose, and BB-8 head to the glamorous city of Canto Bight to find the Master Codebreaker, who can help them sneak onto the First Order Mega-Destroyer. However, before they can do anything, Finn and Rose are captured by Canto Bight police and thrown in jail for leaving their ship on a beach.

## REY
Jedi in Training

**Rey** is a desert scavenger turned Resistance hero. She is strong in the Force but doesn't know the ways of the Jedi. Leia sent Rey on a special mission in a fast ship called the *Millennium Falcon* to find . . .

## LUKE SKYWALKER
The Last Jedi

**Luke Skywalker!** Luke is the last remaining Jedi Master in the galaxy and also Leia's brother.

Rey finds Luke on the remote planet Ahch-To and offers him his old lightsaber, but he tosses it aside! Rey follows Luke all over the island, begging him to return with her to help the Resistance, but Luke refuses to leave.

# CHEWBACCA

*Millennium Falcon* Copilot

**Chewbacca** the Wookiee is Rey's copilot and an old friend of Luke's. He makes some *new* friends on the island, too. Curious little creatures called **porgs** take a liking to the big, furry Wookiee.

# R2-D2

Astromech Droid

**R2-D2** is Luke's old astromech droid and has joined Rey and Chewbacca on their mission.

Luke is surprised to see R2-D2. Like Rey, R2-D2 asks Luke to return with them to help the Resistance. But Luke still refuses. Then R2-D2 shows Luke an old hologram of Leia asking for help, the very hologram that set Luke on the course of his life so many years ago.

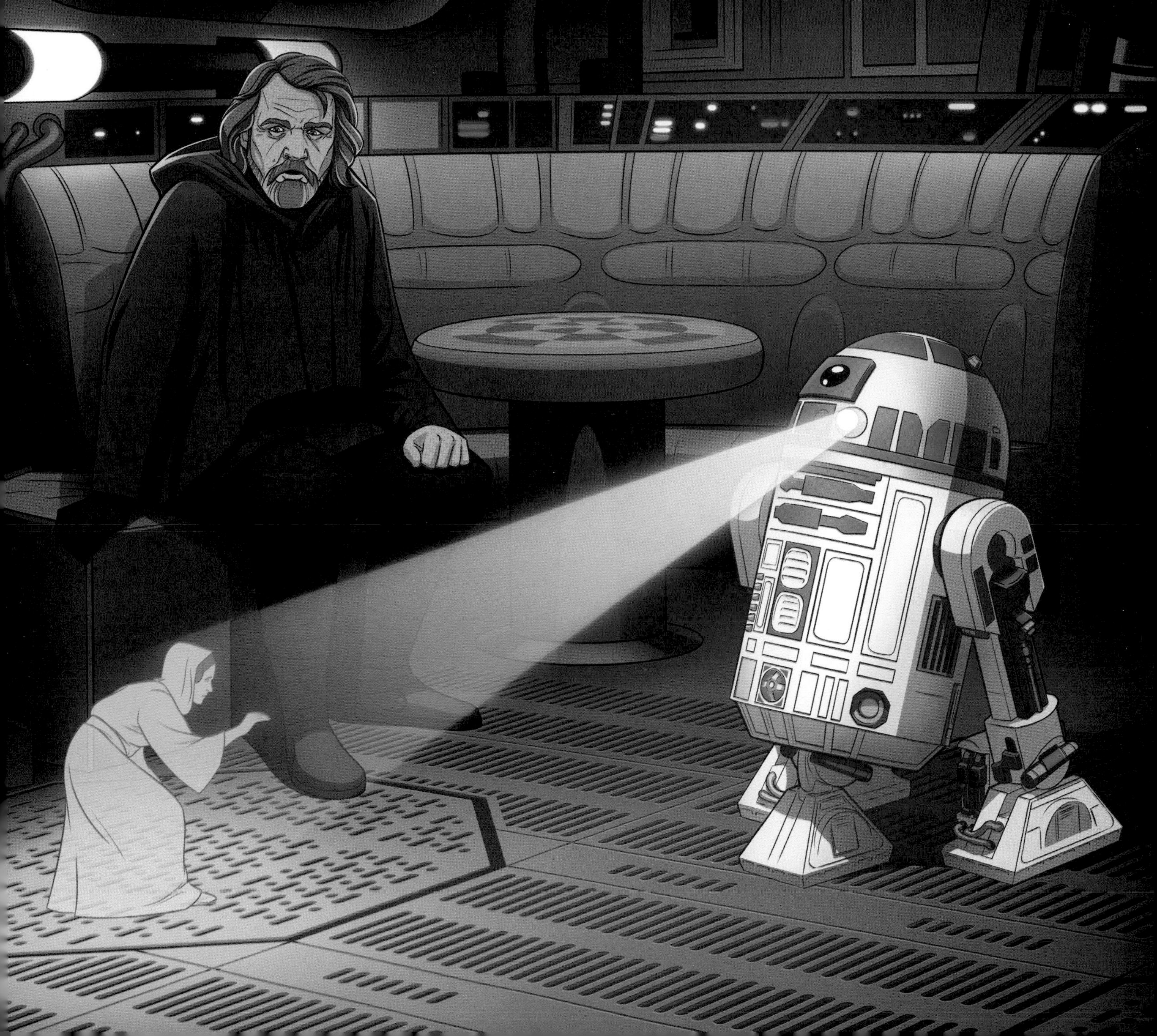

After seeing Leia's original hologram, Luke decides to help the Resistance by training Rey in the Force. Rey thinks that Kylo could still return to the light side of the Force, but Luke disagrees. Rey asks one more time for Luke to return with her to help the Resistance, but he refuses again, so she leaves with Chewbacca and R2-D2.

## FATHIERS
Racing Creatures

**Fathiers** are fast, horselike creatures. Finn and Rose jump on the back of a fathier and race through the streets of Canto Bight. Finn and Rose rejoin DJ and BB-8, and they blast off in a stolen ship and head for the First Order's Mega-Destroyer.

## DJ
Codebreaker

**DJ** is a codebreaker. Finn and Rose meet DJ in their cell on Canto Bight. DJ helps them escape from jail and promises to sneak them on board the First Order's Mega-Destroyer, for the right price.

# CAPTAIN PHASMA

Stormtrooper Commander

**Captain Phasma** is the leader of the First Order's army and Finn's former commander. Finn, Rose, BB-8, and DJ manage to sneak onto the First Order ship, but Captain Phasma captures them before they can deactivate the tracking device.

# GENERAL HUX

First Order Officer

**General Hux**, an officer of the First Order, pays DJ for information about the Resistance's plans and then lets him go free. But Finn and Rose are in trouble!

Suddenly, BB-8 starts blasting stormtroopers from an AT-ST walker. Finn uses the distraction to battle Phasma.

Then, in all the chaos, Finn, Rose, and BB-8 escape from the Mega-Destroyer in a stolen First Order shuttle.

# SUPREME LEADER SNOKE

First Order Leader

**Supreme Leader Snoke** is the leader of the First Order and Kylo Ren's evil master. Rey arrives on the Mega-Destroyer to try to convince Kylo to turn away from the dark side and join her. But Kylo brings her before Snoke instead.

THE LAST JEDI

# ELITE PRAETORIAN GUARD

Snoke's Personal Guard

The deadly **Elite Praetorian Guard** stand beside Snoke, protecting him at all times. But when Snoke asks Kylo to defeat Rey, Kylo tricks his master and defeats Snoke instead!

Rey and Kylo jump into action, fighting Snoke's guards back to back! Rey is thrilled that Kylo has defeated Snoke and has seemingly left the dark side behind. But after they finish fighting the guards, it is clear that Kylo has no intention of leaving the First Order. Instead, he plans to lead it, and he wants Rey to join *him*.

## YODA
Jedi Master

**Yoda** is a Jedi Master and Luke's former teacher. Yoda appears to Luke through the Force. He encourages Luke to do what he can to help Rey and the Resistance.

## VICE ADMIRAL HOLDO
Resistance Leader

**Vice Admiral Holdo** is a leader of the Resistance and friend of Leia's. Holdo crashes a Resistance cruiser through the Mega-Destroyer while the remaining Resistance troops escape to the nearby planet Crait. The crash also allows Rey to flee from Kylo!

The Resistance is trapped on the planet Crait, but having regained her strength, Leia refuses to give up hope. Resistance pilots climb into old ski speeders and battle the First Order across the salt-covered red planet.

Suddenly, Luke appears on the battlefield, allowing the Resistance fighters to retreat back into an old rebel base for safety. Kylo battles Luke, but the old Jedi dodges every swipe of Kylo's powerful red lightsaber. When Kylo finally strikes a blow, it goes right through Luke! Luke starts to disappear, and Kylo understands it was all a distraction so the Resistance could get away. Luke never left Ahch-To. He has used all his energy projecting himself on Crait. He has done what he can to help, and now he is at peace and one with the Force.